SHONEN JUMP'S

Yu-Gi-Oh! GX

NIGHTSHROUD'S SECRET

SHONEN JUMP'S

Yu-Gi-Oh! GX

NIGHTSHROUD'S SECRET

Adapted by Tracey West

SCHOLASTIC INC.

New York Toronto London Auckland Sydney
Mexico City New Delhi Hong Kong Buenos Aires

ISBN-13: 978-0-545-04406-6
ISBN-10: 0-545-04406-5

Published by Scholastic Inc.
SCHOLASTIC and associated logos are trademarks and/or registered trademarks of Scholastic Inc.

12 11 10 9 8 7 6 5 4 3 2 1   8 9 10 11 12/0

Printed in the U.S.A.
First printing, February 2008

SHONEN JUMP'S

Yu-Gi-Oh! GX

NIGHTSHROUD'S SECRET

◆ CHAPTER ONE ◆

SHADOWS FROM THE PAST

A thunderstorm raged across Academy Island. Jagged streaks of lightning illuminated the night sky.

Alexis sat next to her brother's bed. Atticus had been asleep ever since he lost his duel with Jaden — when he was known as the Shadow Rider Nightshroud.

"Only two Shadow Duelists are left," Alexis said softly. "And victory finally seems near. But it would mean so much more if my brother were here with me. His body *and* his mind. Like it used to be . . ."

Alexis's mind wandered back to a time when she was a little girl. She had looked up to her older brother so much! He was always there to offer her good advice.

Alexis had been sitting under a tall tree, looking at

her Duel Monsters cards. She was looking at the high level monsters in her deck.

"Hey, some tough cards," Atticus had said. "But dueling's about more than power."

"What do you mean?" Alexis asked.

"What I mean, is that you need a good purpose for dueling," Atticus said gently. "A reason. That's what really matters in a match."

Alexis sighed and looked at her brother's sleeping face. She could definitely use his advice now.

Suddenly, a deep voice echoed through the dark hospital room.

"You miss him, but there is a way to get him back."

Alexis turned, startled. She had heard that voice before.

A small black cloud hovered in the air behind her.

"Come with me," said the voice. "And I'll give Atticus

back all his memories. If you can defeat me in a duel, that is . . ."

Alexis gasped. A man pretending to be a Shadow Duelist had once kidnapped her, trying to lure Jaden into a duel. Jaden had defeated him. Could he be back?

"At the place we first met . . . the abandoned dorm!" the voice said.

Alexis stood up as if she were hyptonized. She had been searching the old dorm, looking for her missing brother, when the fake Shadow Duelist had found her.

She watched, frozen, as the duelist began to take shape through the cloud. He was a tall man with a dark coat and a round-brimmed hat.

The duelist enveloped her in his cloud of darkness. Alexis didn't protest. The man said he could help her brother. She had to know more . . .

Atticus woke from his bed with a start. "What's going on?" he groaned.

• CHAPTER TWO •

A DEAL IS MADE

The spirit of the card Winged Kuriboh fluttered around Jaden's sleeping head. He brushed it away.

"No wake . . . must sleep more," he muttered.

But Winged Kuriboh wouldn't stop. Then somebody began banging loudly on the door.

Chumley slowly climbed down from his top bunk. "Okay, already! I'm coming!"

Chumley rubbed his eyes and opened the door. Chazz stood there, looking exhausted and angry. The spirits of the Ojama Trio floated around him.

Chumley gasped at the sight of Chazz's tired face.

"What's with you?" Syrus asked from his bunk bed.

"No sleep," Chazz said. "Because of the news I just heard."

"What is it?" Jaden asked.

Moments later they were running through the halls of the medical center. Syrus's brother Zane and Professor Crowler waited for them in front of Atticus's door.

"So?" Jaden asked.

"There's no sign of Alexis," Zane said. "It's like she just disappeared."

"I don't understand. It's not like Alexis to up and vanish," Crowler said. "Maybe her brother knows her whereabouts."

Crowler opened the door to reveal Atticus sprawled face down on the floor.

"Atticus!" Jaden cried.

They ran to his side. Zane lifted him up.

"What happened here?" Zane asked.

Atticus struggled to speak. "It . . . was . . . Titan."

"Who is Titan?" Jaden wondered aloud.

Atticus couldn't say much more. But he did remember where Titan had taken his sister. . . .

. . . Alexis's eyes took in the dim light in the abandoned dorm. Titan led her to the basement, a huge open space with stone floors and stone walls. A dueling circle had been carved into the stone, with a circle for each duelist to stand in on either side. Strange symbols had been carved all around the arena.

Alexis and Titan faced off across the field. Alexis noticed that her opponent wore a mask that covered the top half of his face. A strange eye emblem had been placed in the center of the mask, between Titan's eyes.

"All right, so we duel," Alexis said bravely. "If I win, you restore my brother's memory. That's the deal!"

"Your end of it, at least," Titan replied. "But if I win, I get something, too. Your Spirit Key — and your soul, to take back with me to the Shadow Realm."

Titan grinned. "You see, dear, when you and I first met up, I was but a charlatan of the shadows. However, since being taken in by them, I am now the real deal. An authentic Shadow Rider!"

Alexis studied Titan. Was he telling the truth this time? If this really was a Shadow Game, she would feel every attack launched at her as though it were real. And she could lose her soul in the process.

"Let us begin!" Titan cried.

Just then, Jaden and the others ran into the duel arena. Zane and Chumley supported Atticus between them.

"They're gonna duel!" Chumley said, alarmed.

"And how!" Jaden said. "Alexis, we're here for you. Now beat this creep!"

Alexis turned, surprised and happy to see her friends — and her brother.

"All right, Atticus," she said firmly. "This one's for you!"

• CHAPTER THREE •

DARK ARENA

Alexis and Titan faced each other.

"Let's duel!" they yelled.

"Ready yourself for the shadows," said Titan, making the first move. "I summon Picador Fiend in attack mode!"

A hideous shadow creature appeared on the field. A skeletal beast with a long tail and curved horns carried a creepy-looking rider on its back. The rider's face was a mask with an eerie smile, and two large skulls sat on each of its shoulders. Red and white wings grew from the rider's back. The monster had 1600 attack points.

"Then I'll place one facedown and end my turn," Titan said.

"But not your troubles!" Alexis told him. "I summon Cyber Tutu!"

A monster dressed like a ballet dancer in a tutu appeared, twirling on her pointed ballet shoes. She had short red hair, clear blue goggles, and 1000 attack points.

Titan snorted. "I thought we were dueling, not playing dollies."

"Yeah, well, this so-called dolly is about to play havoc with your life points!" Alexis called back.

Titan nodded. Alexis was right. He was about to lose life points. Unless . . .

I would be in trouble, if I didn't have a facedown on the field that'll activate and destroy that Cyber Tutu as soon as she attacks with her! Titan thought.

Alexis was about to have Cyber Tutu attack, but she hesitated. Titan did have a facedown on the field. It could mean trouble. She decided on another move.

"I play Allegro Toile!" she cried, holding up another card. "It gives my ballerina a little extra kick by destroying one trap or spell card on the field!"

Cyber Tutu's ballet shoes glowed with light. She seemed to fly across the field, her right leg outstretched. It tore into Titan's facedown card. The card vanished.

"No!" Titan cried.

"Now Cyber Tutu can take the lead in this dance, and in the duel, too," Alexis said. "Because Cyber Tutu can attack you directly!"

Cyber Tutu leapt across the field again, twirling in the air as she went.

Slam! Her foot connected with Titan's head. He groaned and fell to his knees as his life points dropped to 3000.

"Next, I play a facedown and end my turn," Alexis said.

"Hey, Alexis is winning!" Syrus remarked.

"It's true," Zane said. "So far, her resolve to win for Atticus has proven stronger than Titan's shadow creatures."

"Well, we'll just see about that!" Titan said. "Now, Picador Fiend, attack Cyber Tutu!"

The shadow beast galloped across the field. A green light glowed in one of the skulls on the creature's shoulder. But before the monster could attack, Alexis held up her hand.

"Sorry!" she cried. She turned up her facedown card. "Go, Doble Passe! Now, I take the attack instead of Cyber Tutu!"

The glowing green ball of energy burst from the skull. Alexis stepped forward to receive the blast. The force of the impact sent her stumbling backwards, and she cringed. Her life points dropped down to 2400.

Her friends looked on, shocked. Why would Alexis

take the attack instead of letting her monster take it? Titan looked shocked, too.

Alexis knew what he was thinking. "Why'd I do it? Because now, *you* have to take a direct hit from Cyber Tutu!"

"What the —" Titan couldn't believe it.

"Go, Pounding Pirouette!" Alexis shouted.

Cyber Tutu twirled across the field once again. *Whack!* Her outstretched leg hit Titan squarely in the face. His life points fell to 2000.

"All right! You show him, Alexis!" Jaden cheered. "She's kickin' butt!"

"It's a long duel, Jaden," Zane said solemnly. He knew how difficult a Shadow Duel could be. He had fought one of the Shadow Riders himself — and lost. "Don't start celebrating yet."

"Yeah, what are you trying to do? Jinx her or something?" Chazz complained.

Jaden shrugged. He had complete faith in Alexis. "Sorry."

Alexis contemplated her strategy. *So far so good,* she thought. *I just need to give him a few more of those combo attacks, and . . .*

Across the field, Titan chuckled maliciously.

"Now what?" Alexis asked him.

"Oh, I'm just remembering our first encounter," he said. "My, how the tables have turned."

"You got that right," Alexis shot back. "Now I'm not just some victim that got kidnapped and stuffed in a coffin! Now I can fight back!"

"No, dear," Titan corrected her. "Before, you were the bait luring my prey to me. But now, you're the one who's my target. And now, dear, I'm going to treat you as such. I play Ritual of the Matador!"

Titan pulled a card from his hand. Then he pulled another.

"Next, I sacrifice the Level 6 Summoned Skull in order to summon . . . Matador Fiend!" he said dramatically.

A monster in a gray costume appeared. A mask covered most of his face, and his hands and feet were large, sharp claws. Alexis was surprised to see his stats: zero attack and defense points!

"Something tells me there's more to him than meets the eye," she muttered thoughtfully.

"Oh, there is, so keep a sharp lookout," Titan advised. "Though that may be difficult for you after I play this. I activate Dark Arena!"

Titan's strange face mask glowed as he activated

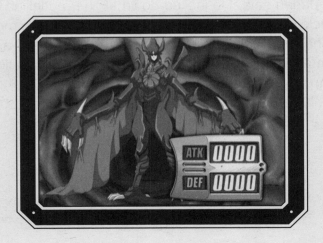

the card, a field spell. The entire circular field plunged into pitch-black darkness, an unearthly darkness that no light could penetrate.

"I can't see!" Alexis cried, panicked. She could barely make out Cyber Tutu in front of her, and she couldn't see Titan and his monsters at all.

How can I fight if I can't make out my enemies? she asked herself.

Titan just laughed. "Your move!" he called out.

Just outside the field, Jaden and the others marveled at the field spell. They could still see fine all around them, but it was like a dark cloud had descended on the field. They couldn't see anything at all in the inky blackness.

"Someone should go in there," Crowler said. "Someone other than me, of course."

"Jaden, you took this guy on in a duel before," Chazz pointed out. "Tell Alexis how to get out of this jam!"

"Wish I could, but something tells me he's different now," Jaden said. He looked down at the medallion around his neck. He and Atticus had each won half of the medallion in a Shadow Duel. Together, the two pieces were a kind of charm against the Shadow Realm. Now the medallion was glowing brightly. Jaden knew what that meant.

"The guy I dueled was a fake. But this time, his powers are *real*!"

• CHAPTER FOUR •

ATTACK OF THE FIENDS

Alexis couldn't see Titan, but she could hear his deep laughter across the dueling field.

"The darkness is fitting for a Shadow Duel, don't you think?" he asked. "But still, allow me to shed at least *some* light on the situation. Here, in the dark arena, your monsters in attack mode *must* attack. But since they can't see, I am allowed to choose their target for them."

That didn't worry Alexis. "Just because my monsters can't see doesn't mean we can't win," she said. "I'll just need someone who packs a really powerful punch. My draw!"

Alexis took a card from her Duel Disk. She held it out.

"I activate the spell card Polymerization!" she called

out. "Fusing Etoile Cyber and Blade Skater to create Cyber Blader!"

Two of the monsters in Alexis's hand fused together to form a new warrior. Cyber Blader wore a red and gray uniform. Long black hair swung down her back, and a red mask covered part of her face. She had 2100 attack points.

"What's cool about her is that her special effect changes with the number of monsters you have," Alexis explained. "Since you have two monsters out on the field, Cyber Blader's attack points are doubled to 4200!"

But Titan just laughed, even though 4200 attack points was nothing to laugh at.

"Whatever will I do?" he wondered aloud.

"You'll get your butt kicked!" Alexis told him. "'Cause it doesn't matter now who I attack. My Blader's the strongest creature out! She'll take down any target."

Alexis pointed to her Cyber Blader. "Go in!"

Cyber Blader raced across the field, spinning around and around like a whirlwind.

"Face her, Matador Fiend!" Titan cried.

"Go, Whirlwind Rage!" Alexis yelled.

Cyber Blader slammed into Matador Fiend. Alexis waited to hear the monster's cries of defeat, but nothing happened.

Instead, a green light came from Matador Fiend's head. The light slammed into Cyber Blader, shattering her!

Alexis didn't see any of this, but she heard her monster being destroyed.

"My Cyber Blader is so much stronger than Matador Fiend!" she protested. "She should win this! What's going on?"

"Oh, I'm so sorry," Titan said, with fake sympathy in his voice. "Didn't you know? Matador Fiend cannot be destroyed in battle, and it also doesn't take damage. Although the monster that battles it is destroyed!"

"No way," Alexis said in disbelief. That meant every time she sent out a monster, Titan would make it attack Matador Fiend. And she would lose it!

"There's more," Titan said. "Just like I said before, every monster that's in attack mode here must now battle each other."

"I don't think so!" Alexis countered. "Cyber Tutu's special ability allows her to attack you directly! So your Matador Fiend will have to pick a fight with someone else."

"You're wrong again," Titan replied. "Cyber Tutu's special ability only activates if there are no monsters on my field with less attack points. But my Matador Fiend has *zero* attack points. So you see, Cyber Tutu's effect can't be used. Nor will it ever be used again, once Picador Fiend gets done with her!"

Alexis gasped. Titan was right.

"This will be her last dance," Titan promised.

Picador Fiend advanced across the field. Another ball of green energy formed in one of the skull heads. The light slammed into Cyber Tutu, shattering her.

"Tutu!" Alexis cried. The light hit Alexis next, and her life points dropped to 1800.

"So this is what a Shadow Game feels like," she said, gritting her teeth.

"Don't worry, Alexis," Titan said, chuckling. "At least your brother won't remember that you failed him."

"I'm not gong to fail him!" she said, her voice filled with determination. "I play Cyber Gymnast in defense mode!"

As the monster appeared, 1800 defense points flashed. A sleek figure in a gray leotard, she wore a white mask that covered her face. Spikes rose from her arms.

"Give me your best shot," Alexis said.

"Dear, if you actually knew what my best was, I doubt that you would be so eager for it," Titan said. "Haven't you realized yet? I'm not the same duelist you knew from before. I changed when the shadows took me in."

When Titan had lost his duel with Jaden, real fiends from the Shadow Realm had come to claim him. He cried out for someone to help him, and a voice answered him in the blackness.

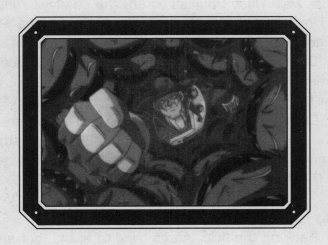

"I will spare you the agony of the shadows, and you will be my devoted servant," the voice said. "You will do my bidding."

Titan had agreed, and his dark master had given him the facemask in return. The mask gave Titan all the powers of the Shadow Realm.

"Now I am more powerful than ever!" Titan bragged to Alexis.

"And uglier," Alexis said. "But I got news for you, true

dueling power doesn't come from some shadow charm. It comes from the reasons *why* you duel. And that's why you're going to lose this. Got it?"

"The reasons why you duel? Where did that come from? Surely not from your beloved brother," Titan taunted her. "After all, the whole reason he became a Shadow Rider was to gain power."

"That's not true!" Alexis cried. "You're a liar!"

"It's a fact," Titan said. "But if you still don't believe me, just wait! Once I banish you to the shadows, you'll see what I mean. And you'll see soon. Because the Picador Fiend now attacks you directly!"

Green light shot from the skull of Picador Fiend, and this time, Alexis took the full force of the attack. She cried out and fell to her knees as her life points plummeted to 200.

Outside the dueling field, Jaden and the others heard Alexis's screams. Veins of purple light pulsated on the darkness covering the field. Atticus reached out his hand to touch them, clearly worried about his sister.

"I know it's tough, Atticus," Jaden said. "We just have to hope she's okay."

Back on the field, Alexis tried to stand, but she was too weak.

"The end is near. The shadows beckon," Titan warned. "You squirm but they still close in. It is simply a matter of time now."

Alexis tried to plan her next move. *With Cyber Gymnast's special ability, I can discard one card from my hand and destroy one of his monsters,* she thought. It was the only way to get rid of Matador Fiend. *But since I don't*

have any cards right now I'll have to wait until the next round to use it.

"What are you plotting over there?" Titan asked. "Let me guess. Something with Cyber Gymnast? Well, don't even bother. She won't be around for much longer! I summon Banderillero Fiend!"

A monster with a brown, snakelike body flashed onto the field. It had a wide mouth filled with sharp fangs, glowing red eyes, and leathery wings. The creature had 900 attack points.

"His special ability destroys Cyber Gymnast!" Titan cried.

Banderillero Fiend glowed green, and Cyber Gymnast shattered across the field — along with Alexis's hopes.

"Get up!" Titan called out. "Or are your reasons for dueling not enough anymore?"

Alexis was mortified. She had no monsters in her hand and only 200 life points.

Maybe he's right, Alexis thought. *Maybe my reasons aren't enough. Because as much as I want to win this, I simply don't have the strength. It's over. My key . . . my brother . . . my soul . . . I've lost them all!*

Then she collapsed.

• CHAPTER FIVE •

CYBER BLADER RETURNS

"That's right, stay down," Titan said, pleased. "After all, the reasons you fight aren't nearly as strong as the shadows."

Alexis felt as though she couldn't move, like she would never get up.

And then she heard it.

"*Alexis . . .*"

It was Atticus! His voice pierced through the darkness. Alexis stirred.

"Don't give up!" her brother's voice was stronger now. "You can do this!"

Alexis slowly rose back to her feet. Atticus was her reason for dueling. It was the only reason she needed.

"What's this?" Titan asked, surprised.

"*This* is my turn!" Alexis said, drawing a card from her Duel Disk. She held it up. "And I activate Pot of Greed! So now I get to draw two more new cards."

Alexis drew and examined the cards in her hand. They were just what she needed.

"I play The Warrior Returning Alive to bring back Blade Skater to my hand!" she announced.

The card featuring the silver skater returned.

"Then I'll activate the spell card Fusion Recovery," Alexis continued. "It allows me to bring back Polymerization and Etoile Cyber from my graveyard."

"What?" Titan asked in disbelief. He knew what was coming.

"Next I'll activate Polymerization and fuse together Etoile Cyber and Blade Skater to summon Cyber Blader!" Alexis announced triumphantly. "You remember her? Well, now she's back and ready to get some sweet revenge!"

Alexis felt her confidence rising. "This is over! Your shadow powers have failed you. You've lost the duel."

"You're delirious," said Titan. "I still have three monsters out. And you are still in the dark."

"Yeah, maybe, but not for long," Alexis said. "Because my Cyber Blader's about to light up your world."

"You lie!" Titan cried.

"Wrong," Alexis said. "Since you have three monsters on the field, Blader's special ability Shining Cyber Light activates, canceling any and all effects you have out!"

Cyber Blader's body shone with white light. The light expanded throughout the arena, shattering the darkness as though it were glass.

"No fair! You've destroyed my spell!" Titan wailed.

The darkness disappeared completely. Jaden and the others could see Alexis clearly once again. And Alexis could see Titan's face — and it looked frightened.

"And there's more," Alexis said. "Matador Fiend's special ability to reduce his battle damage to zero is negated, too!"

"No!" Titan yelled.

"So go, Cyber Blader!" Alexis yelled. "Attack with Skate Blade Slash!"

Cyber Blader raced across the field once again. This time, she hit Matador Fiend with a powerful kick. The monster exploded in pieces.

Next she aimed a kick right at Titan. The Shadow Rider screamed as his life points dropped from 2000 all the way to zero in one blow.

As soon as he lost, strange, sludgelike creatures

emerged from beneath the field. They crawled all over Titan, covering his body with their dark gray forms.

"No, not again!" Titan screamed.

Then Titan and the creatures vanished. All that was left of Titan was his mask.

The friends left the dark basement of the abandoned dorm and stood outside in the morning sunlight. Alexis and Atticus hugged each other.

"Addy, welcome back!" Alexis said tearfully. That bright spark was back in her brother's eyes. He had regained all of his memories!

"Thanks, Lex, for everything," he said.

"But wait," Alexis said. "There are so many unanswered questions, like how did you ever end up in the Shadow Realm? Titan said you did it for the power."

"Believe me, Lexie, I never chose to go," Atticus said. "One day a few of us were told to meet at the abandoned dorm. There was supposed to be a duel test in the base-ment. But instead, we found hundreds of those little shadow fiends. I couldn't escape."

Alexis gasped. It sounded horrible!

"I was then brought to the Shadow Realm," he explained. "And kept there. For months they brainwashed me until I became this thing called Nightshroud."

"But who?" Alexis asked. "Who was it that brain-washed you?"

Atticus shook his head. "I never did figure that out," he replied. "However, the person who called me to take the duel test was . . . Professor Banner!"

Everyone listening gasped, their eyes wide with disbelief.

"Our Professor Banner?" Jaden asked, unbelieving. Professor Banner was the friendliest teacher at Duel Academy. Not to mention he was a Key Keeper, charged

with protecting the Spirit Gates. But if he had sent Atticus to that duel test, it could mean only one thing . . .

"He's in on it," Jaden said solemnly.

Could it really be true? Jaden wasn't sure.

But if it was, they were all in danger!

CHAPTER SIX

WHERE'S BANNER?

Rays of morning sunlight glittered on the blue waters surrounding Academy Island. All over the island, young students learning the art of battling with Duel Monsters were awake, dressed and heading for class.

Well, except for three students, that is . . .

Jaden, Syrus, and Chumley raced from their room in the Slifer Red dorm.

"We overslept!" shrieked Syrus.

"Which means we missed . . . breakfast!" moaned Chumley.

They ran into the dorm's dining hall and headed straight for their usual table. Their breakfast trays were there, waiting for them.

"Whew, there's some left!" said Jaden, who hated to miss a meal almost as much as Chumley did.

"Let's dig in," Syrus suggested.

But when Jaden picked up his cereal bowl, he saw that it was empty.

He frowned. "Not that much to dig into."

"Someone's cleared off our trays!" Syrus cried.

Chumley groaned. "What kind of selfish slime would do that?"

Then the boys heard a snicker from across the room. They looked up and saw someone they hadn't noticed before.

"You snooze, you lose," said Chazz.

Even though he lived in the Slifer Red dorm, Chazz wore a black uniform. Once a top student at the academy, Chazz had left for a while, and had been working his way back to the top ever since he returned. He and Jaden had been fierce rivals, but lately, they'd been working together to stop the Shadow Riders from taking over the world.

Right now, though, Syrus was furious with Chazz.

"Give us back our food or I'm telling!" he demanded.

Chazz leaned back in his chair and smiled. "I would give it back, only I ate it all," he said. "And it was gooooood!"

Syrus cried out, "Professor!"

"Banner!" Chumley yelled.

"Chazz is being Chazz again!" Jaden added.

The three friends waited for Professor Banner to come to the scene, like he always did. Banner was in charge of the Slifer Red dorm, and even though he was mild-mannered — and a little weird, some thought — he did a good job of keeping everyone in line.

But Professor Banner didn't answer them. In fact, there was no sign of him in the dining room at all.

Jaden frowned. Banner hadn't been around lately, which worried Jaden. Atticus's accusation that Banner was somehow involved with the Shadow Realm still haunted him. He couldn't believe that Banner was evil — but maybe he was in trouble, somehow.

"Don't tell me Banner's still MIA," Jaden muttered. "This is getting serious!"

• CHAPTER SEVEN •

THE SEARCH BEGINS

The boys made it to their first class without food — and without any news about Professor Banner. They sat in their usual seats in the huge, dome-shaped classroom with a large group of other students from all three dorms: Slifer Red, Ra Yellow, and Obelisk Blue. The students faced a large screen on the wall and a teacher's desk in front of the screen.

Right now, the desk — Professor Banner's — was empty.

Jaden rested his head in his hands and sighed.

"It'll be okay, Jaden," Syrus consoled him.

"Yeah, totally," Chumley chimed in. "Chancellor Sheppard has a whole crew of people looking for Professor Banner. They'll find him."

"It's just a matter of time," Syrus added.

Jaden sighed. "I hope."

Chumley pointed to the empty desk. "On the bright side, at least we get a break from class."

But just then, Professor Crowler walked into the classroom, chuckling. Every student in the room moaned quietly.

Crowler was a stuffy, arrogant teacher who added frilly lace to his Obelisk Blue uniform. He had spent the beginning of the year trying to find someone who could bring down Jaden in a duel.

"Good morning, students. Guess what?" Crowler said, in a falsely cheerful voice. "Due to Professor Banner's absence, I will be your substitute teacher for the day! Aren't you lucky?"

More quiet moans filled the room.

"Because I'm not!" Crowler continued, his voice changing to a cranky tone. "It was *supposed* to be my day off!"

Crowler sat down at Banner's desk and slammed a pile of thick, old books onto the table. He pressed a button on the desk, and a picture of a strange symbol appeared on the big screen behind him. It looked like an incomplete circle with a big dot in the center.

"Let's see, the Mark of Amnael," Crowler muttered. He opened a book and began to leaf through the pages. "Yes, that's where Professor Banner left off. More Duel Academy nonsense, I'm sure. Well, according to these tomes, the basics of this are . . . well, that doesn't make any sense. Pure rubbish! Useless prattle!"

"Oh boy," Jaden whispered. "He hates this stuff."

But Syrus smiled. "No, it's not that, Jay," he said. "I think he just doesn't get any of it himself!"

Now Crowler was setting up science equipment on the desk. He took a length of wire and bent it into a shape resembling the Mark of Amnael. Then he filled a glass beaker with a clear, bubbling liquid.

"Now, let's see here," he said. "I think this is right."

Crowler dipped the wire symbol into the liquid.

Bam! A small explosion rocked Crowler's desk, covering him with clouds of gray smoke. When the smoke cleared, the students could see the wire symbol stuck to Crowler's forehead.

"Aaah! Hot! Hot! Hot!" Crowler cried. He removed the wire — and the Mark of Amnael was burned into his forehead.

Jaden shook his head. "Boy, I sure wish Professor Banner would show up soon."

"Of course, Banner usually blew himself up, too," Syrus pointed out.

"True," Jaden admitted.

Then Crowler's grating voice interrupted him.

"Mr. Slifer Slacker!" the professor cried out.

"Uh, yes, sir?" Jaden asked.

"Chancellor Sheppard would like a word," Crowler said.

"Me?" Jaden asked. When Sheppard wanted to see you, it was serious.

"That's right. You and the rest of the gang," Crowler said. He nodded at Chazz, Syrus, and Chumley, as well as two other students: Alexis and Bastion. "Report to him at once!"

Minutes later, Jaden was standing in Chancellor Sheppard's office. He was an imposing figure with a bald head and a gray beard and mustache. Sheppard sat behind his large desk. Everyone from Crowler's class was gathered around him, including Crowler, and one more student: Syrus's older brother, Zane. All of the Key Keepers were present — except for Professor Banner.

Jaden looked around the group. So far, Zane, Bastion, and Professor Crowler had lost their keys. Jaden had battled several Shadow Riders himself. His first encounter had almost cost him his life. The duels were extremely dangerous — but he hadn't lost one yet.

"What do you mean he's still lost?" Jaden asked, after Chancellor Sheppard updated them. "Professor Banner couldn't just have vanished into thin air, could he?"

"Who knows?" Sheppard said sadly. "The bottom line is we've looked everywhere and can't find him."

"And there's no log of his leaving the island," Dr. Crowler added.

"So then, I think we all know what happened," Chazz said. "Banner got sucked into the shadows!"

"Don't say that!" Alexis cried, her pale eyes wide with alarm. Getting taken into the Shadow World was a horrible price to pay for losing a Shadow Duel.

Sheppard shook his head. "No," he said. "If he lost a Shadow Game, a Spirit Gate would have opened. But there's been no new activity."

"Still, I have a feeling the Shadow Riders have something to do with all of this," Jaden mused.

After the meeting, Jaden talked with Syrus and Chumley outside.

"We've got to find out what happened," Jaden said.

"How do we find out what's up if we can't even find Banner?" Chumley said glumly. "*Or* another breakfast."

"You know, Chumley's got a point," Syrus said. "After all, Chancellor Sheppard turned all of Duel Academy inside out!"

"What can the three of us do that hasn't already been done?" Chumley added.

Jaden took a deep breath. "Look, guys, I know it seems hopeless right now. But we can't give up!" he said. "We owe it to Banner to keep looking. He'd do the same thing for us. Right?

"Right!"

The boys looked up to see Chazz standing there, a confident grin on his face.

"Beat it, Chazz!" Syrus warned.

"Chill. I'm not here to cause trouble. I'm here . . ." Chazz paused dramatically. "To save the day! To find Professor Banner!"

Jaden groaned. When Chazz decided to play detective, there was no stopping him.

The boys followed Chazz as he led them all over Academy Island.

"When searching for a missing person, the first thing you have to do is go to the scene of the crime," Chazz said in his most professional voice.

"But we don't know *where* that is!" Syrus said. "Isn't that the problem? Isn't it?"

Jaden chuckled.

Chazz turned toward them, frustrated. "Look! It's a figure of speech!"

"Now come on," he continued, turning back around. "We just have to retrace Banner's steps."

Syrus sighed. "We don't *know* his steps."

"I know," Jaden said. "But let's just humor him."

"Can I just laugh at him instead?" Syrus pleaded.

"Quiet!" Chazz ordered. "Chazz is on the job!"

• CHAPTER EIGHT •

A CLUE!

Chazz led the search party to Professor Banner's office. The boys opened drawers and rummaged through bookshelves.

"Well, guys, there are no clues here," Syrus said.

"Yeah, you'd think he'd leave a note or something!" Jaden said.

"He did!" Chumley cried. He was on his hands and knees, checking the bottom shelf of a telephone table. He held up a white piece of paper.

Jaden took the paper from him and studied it.

"It's Professor Banner's handwriting, and it's not very clear," he said, frowning. "Something about a tree?"

"Must be a code," Chazz said, in his best detective voice.

Chazz took the paper and knelt on the floor to examine it more closely. Jaden, Syrus, and Chumley gathered around him.

"Of course, I see," Chazz said.

"You see what, Chazz?" Jaden asked, exasperated.

"The clue," Chazz replied. "See, Jaden. *Tree* must have a secret meaning."

Syrus was skeptical. "Really?"

"Oh, come on, it's plain as day!" Chazz said. "At least, for a genius such as I."

Chumley was growing impatient with Chazz's dramatics. "Okay! Okay! So what does it mean?"

"What it means" — Chazz once again paused dramatically — "is Banner took on the seventh Shadow Rider!"

"Are you serious?" Jaden asked.

"Of course I am!" Chazz said confidently. "And there's more, too! I know who the rider is as well. Oh man, I am just too good."

"Yeah, you're great," Jaden said dryly. "So then, who is it already?"

"Who, indeed!" Chazz answered. "The note was by the phone. Which means he wrote it while talking to some-one. Someone who's name sounds like *tree*!"

Chazz stood up and paced back and forth across the floor.

"Now then, who do we know whose name sounds like *tree*?" he asked. "A hint? She works in the cafeteria."

Syrus raised an eyebrow. "You mean . . ."

"It's Dorothy!" Chazz cried, "It rhymes with *tree*! She's a Shadow Rider! She's the one who's taken out Professor Banner."

Jaden, Syrus, and Chumley gasped. Dorothy was a plump, sweet lady who was friendly to everyone. Could she really be an evil Shadow Rider?

"She's the one?" Jaden couldn't believe it.

"That's right," Chazz said, "and I'm gonna call her on it."

Chazz called the cafeteria and confronted Dorothy.

"What? Shadow Rider? How do you ride a shadow?" Dorothy asked. "Is this a crank call? I'll star sixty-nine you!"

Chazz hung up, embarrassed. "Okay, so maybe I was just a little off," he admitted.

"A little off!" Jaden, Syrus, and Chumley cried.

Chazz shrugged. "Let's keep digging."

The boys tore apart Banner's office, looking for more clues.

Jaden held up a pair of shoes. "This a clue?"

"Guess again," Chazz said.

Chumley held up some headphones. "How 'bout this?"

Chazz scoffed. "You gotta be kidding!"

They found breakfast crumbs, a ball of lint, and even toenail clippings, but no clues. Until . . .

"Check this out," Syrus said. He held up what looked like a map. The map showed what looked like a forest of trees — and there was a strange symbol in the middle.

"Of course! It's obvious!" Chazz said, but this time he was actually onto something. "Check out that symbol. It's the Mark of Amnael. The one we learned in class."

"You're right!" Jaden said.

"Now, this is a clue. I mean, Banner was about to teach us about the Mark of Amnael. This must be where he is!" He smiled smugly.

"Yeah, and it's in a forest, too," Syrus pointed out.

"One with trees," Jaden added. "Think maybe that's what the note meant?"

The boys left the dorm and went into the wooded area on the outskirts of Academy Island.

"Let the rescue expedition for Professor Banner begin!" Jaden said. "Follow me, guys!"

"Follow you?" Chazz asked. "Yeah, right. I'm the one who figured this whole thing out, so you guys can follow me! If you can keep up, that is."

Jaden, Syrus, and Chumley groaned as Chazz took the lead.

"So, uh, Chazz, other than following you, what's the plan here?" Syrus asked.

"Yeah," Chumley said. "How do we find Banner once we find the alchemy mark?"

"Easy. We find his cat, Pharoah. With this!" Chazz held up a cat toy, a fuzzy ball on the end of a stick.

Jaden looked doubtful.

"Ooh, ooh, I have an idea!" Syrus said. He whipped out a black marker. "Let's try a different route."

Syrus scribbled on Chazz's face. When he was done, Chazz had the whiskers and nose of a cat!

"There! Perfect!" Syrus cried. "Now Pharaoh will think

you're a cat! Of course, you still have to develop a convincing meow."

Chazz's dark eyes grew angry. "How about I show you my claws instead?" he growled.

The boys ran ahead of Chazz, laughing.

"You better run!" Chazz called out.

While Chazz fumed, a hooded figure watched him from a tree. The man wore black pants and a long jacket. His eyes glowed yellow from underneath a mask that covered most of his face.

Then he silently melted into the darkness.

• CHAPTER NINE •

ALEXIS FALLS

Back at the Obelisk Blue dorm, Alexis walked to her room, her mind filled with thoughts. Ever since the Shadow Riders had decided to try to obtain the keys to the seven Spirit Gates, her life had been turned upside down. She had competed in a fierce Shadow Game and won. And she had found her brother, Atticus, who had disappeared mysteriously — and had reappeared as a Shadow Rider.

The evil that had infected Atticus had left him, and he was back to being her brother again. But he was changed by his experience, and still weak. Alexis had been keeping a close eye on him.

When Alexis opened the door to her room, hoping to see her brother, she found the space in disarray. The window had been smashed, furniture broken, and the debris was scattered everywhere.

"Atticus?" Alexis called out, worried. She scanned the room. "No, he's gone!"

As panic rose inside her, something bright and yellow caught her eye. A strange symbol floated in the middle of the mess — the same symbol Crowler had showed in class that day — the Mark of Amnael.

The symbol floated across the room and through the open window. Alexis followed it out onto the balcony. Down below, she saw a figure running, heading into the woods.

She leapt off of the balcony and took off running.

"Where's my brother?" she cried out angrily, but she got no reply. She followed him into the woods until they came to a small clearing. The runner stopped and faced her.

Alexis quickly sized him up. The hood, the mask, the yellow glowing eyes could mean only one thing.

"So let me guess," she said. "You're a Shadow Rider."

The figure nodded. Without speaking, he took out a gray Duel Disk from under his cloak. Alexis knew he wanted to duel.

"Well, let's go!" Alexis said hotly. "Because I know you have Atticus, and I'm not leaving here without him!"

Alexis activated her own Duel Disk. "Now let's duel!" she cried. "Here I come, rider!"

Each duelist started with 4000 life points. They each drew seven cards. Jaden and the others were still searching through the forest, with no idea that Alexis was in trouble. Alexis would have to duel this Shadow Rider without any help from from her friends.

The Shadow Rider made his move, playing only a facedown card. Then Alexis made her move.

"First I play the spell Polymerization and fuse Etoile Cyber with Blade Skater to create Cyber Blader!"

Two Duel Monsters appeared briefly on the field. Then they swirled together, and a Cyber Blader appeared in their place. The red-masked hero had 2100 attack points.

"You picked the wrong Key Keeper to mess with," Alexis said. "Cyber Blader, attack!"

Cyber Blader zoomed across the clearing, aimed right for the Shadow Rider. But before she could reach him, the Shadow Rider's facedown card rose up. Lightning bolts shot from the card, zapping Cyber Blader.

"A trap card?" Alexis was shocked. "So Cyber Blader's attack didn't go through. Not good."

The Shadow Rider silently held up a card.

The clouds overhead parted, revealing a sky streaked

deep orange and yellow. Without warning, jagged meteors fell from the sky, bombarding Alexis and Cyber Blader.

The bright lights in the sky blinded Alexis, and she covered her face. When she opened her eyes, she saw Cyber Blader shattering into pieces — destroyed in one turn.

My Cyber Blader's gone, which means I'm wide open to attack! Alexis realized. She saw that the Shadow Rider had drawn another card.

She gasped as a black dragon with two heads rose up behind the Shadow Rider. The first mouth opened up to reveal a blazing yellow fireball. A blue fireball burned inside the second mouth.

Alexis watched in horror as the dragons reared back their heads to hurl the blazing missiles at her. She knew from her previous Shadow Duel that everything that happened in the duel was real. Even the pain.

"Aaaaaah!" Alexis cried out as a ball of green fire engulfed her, draining all of her life points. She collapsed on the ground, her cards scattered around her.

The Shadow Rider stepped up to her. He reached down and took a key from around her neck — a key that would open one of the Spirit Gates. Then he took an old book out of the folds of his cloak. The Mark of Amnael was set into the book's leather cover.

He opened the book, and the Mark of Amnael shone from it. Alexis's body glowed with the light, and then was absorbed into the book.

The Shadow Rider closed the book and walked back into the forest.

· CHAPTER TEN ·

A PHARAOH IN THE WOODS

Night fell over Academy Island, and Jaden and his friends were still no closer to finding Professor Banner. They built a fire and sat around it, warming their hands.

"We'll find Banner soon, I'm sure!" Syrus said hopefully.

"I hope. Because I really miss him, you know? All the little things he did," Jaden said. "Like that time he gave me his dinner — pork fried rice with chili sauce. My favorite!"

"Course, he is allergic to chili sauce," Chumley pointed out. "But, uh, you know. I guess that had very little to do with it."

"Yeah, I guess so," Jaden said, but there was a tiny bit of doubt in his voice.

"Well, he was always nice to you, Sy, right?" Chumley asked.

"I suppose," Syrus said. "There *was* that time he gave me expired milk at dinner."

"Okay," Chumley agreed. "So he acts a bit weird sometimes."

"Weird? I'll tell you what's weird," Chazz said. "One time he pushed all of his carrots onto my plate! And he said I could repay him by giving him my dessert! He sure is shifty sometimes."

"It's true," Syrus agreed. "Like when he tried to teach me how to swim." Banner had tied a rope around Syrus's waist, given him a spear, and sent him into the bay. "I just ended up spearing his fish for dinner!"

Jaden nodded. "Yeah, I guess he kinda has two sides to him. But that doesn't make him a bad person."

"Yeah," Chazz agreed. "Guess that's why we're looking for him."

Just then, a familiar sound echoed through the woods.

Meow. Meow.

"Pharaoh?" Jaden cried, standing up.

The boys doused their campfire and joined Jaden. Chazz had a flashlight, and he shone it into the trees.

"Here, kitty!" Syrus yelled.

"Come here, cat!" Chumley cried.

Meow. Meow.

The sound seemed to come from all around them.

"Pharaoh is close," Chazz said. "Quick, guys. Let's spread out. This could be our only chance!"

The boys took off in four directions. Chazz stepped into the dark woods.

"Something's wrong! I'm scared!"

Chazz scowled at the sound of the familiar voice. It was Ojama Yellow, the spirit of one of Chazz's Duel Monster cards. Chazz had a special bond with three monsters known

as the Ojama Trio, and their spirits appeared to him —
usually to Chazz's annoyance.

"Get lost," Chazz said.

Ojama Yellow was a small yellow monster with eyes
on the end of long eyestalks. He wrung his hands nervously
and continued to follow Chazz as he went deeper into the
trees.

Chazz followed the mewing sound until he stumbled
upon the cat Pharoah, sleeping on the ground.

"What the —" Chazz began, surprised, but then he
noticed something else. His flashlight revealed a pair of eyeglasses on the ground as well.

Professor Banner's glasses, Chazz realized. *He's
close. Must be.*

A symbol made of yellow light shone in front of the
cat — the Mark of Amnael.

"Whoa," Chazz said. Whatever had happened to
Professor Banner, the Mark of Amnael had something to do
with it.

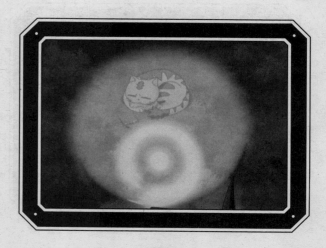

The glowing symbol floated deeper into the woods, and Chazz followed. As he walked, he noticed something else on the ground.

"Hey! There's Banner's necktie, too," Chazz said. "And his shirt. But where's the professor?"

The rest of the Ojama Trio — Ojama Green and Ojama Black — appeared in their spirit form, too.

"Who cares!" they cried, shivering with fear.

Chazz followed the light into a clearing in the woods. The light faded.

Then a masked figure emerged from the trees.

◆ CHAPTER ELEVEN ◆

TIME TO CHAZZ YOU UP!

The Ojama Trio hid behind Chazz.

The masked figure stepped into view. He activated his Duel Disk, and his glowing yellow eyes seemed to burn through Chazz.

But Chazz wasn't afraid.

"You took Banner!" he cried. "Well, I'm gonna win him back!"

Chazz activated his Duel Disk. "Now let's go!"

"Get 'em, Chazz!" cheered Ojama Yellow.

"We're with ya!" cried Ojama Green.

"That's right!" added Ojama Black.

The trio swirled around Chazz. "Time to Chazz you up!"

Chazz stared at the mysterious duelist. He looked
down at his feet to see that a strange puddle of water had
appeared. The water stretched across the clearing, form-
ing the shape of a duel arena. He was sure he was facing
a Shadow Rider.

"Duel!" he cried.

Nearby, Jaden, Syrus, and Chumley heard Pharaoh meow.

"Where's your pal Professor Banner?" Chumley
asked.

Pharaoh mewed in reply.

Then the charm Jaden wore around his neck began
to glow. Jaden gasped. It glowed only when someone from
the Shadow World was near.

Whatever lay ahead, it couldn't be good.

Back in the clearing, both duelists had summoned monsters.

Chazz's Armed Dragon Level 7 stood next to him, a
sturdy, massive monster with 800 attack points.

Two beasts stood behind the Shadow Rider, but they were shrouded in gray mist, and Chazz couldn't make them out. Part of him wondered what powers they had, what they could do to him.

But it didn't matter.

"You're going down, Shadow Rider," Chazz said. "And you know why? 'Cause Chazz is on the job."

Chazz held up a card from his hand.

"I send Despair from the Dark to the graveyard," he announced, throwing down the card. "And activate Armed Dragon's ability! Now all your monsters with equal or fewer attack points than the monster I discarded will be destroyed!"

Chazz turned to his Armed Dragon. "Go! Take them down!"

A ball of light burned in the monster's chest. It flowed like a tidal wave across the watery battlefield, smashing into the Shadow Rider's monsters. They exploded with a horrific cry.

Armed Dragon roared triumphantly.

"And next, I'm going to attack you directly," Chazz said. "Any last words, Shadow Rider, before you're toast?"

The Ojama Trio giggled gleefully.

"I should've never doubted you, boss!" said Ojama Yellow.

Back in the woods, Jaden and his friends searched for Chazz.

"Chazz! Where are you? Hello!" Jaden cried.

"He couldn't have gone far," Syrus said. "Weird."

"Something's wrong," Jaden said, worried. "We should've never split up."

Back on the field, the Shadow Rider drew another card. Chazz watched, horrified, as a giant creature rose up behind the duelist. It was bathed in shadow, so Chazz couldn't see what it looked like. But he knew he had never seen anything like it.

What is that thing? Chazz asked himself.

The Shadow Rider silently put another card in his Duel Disk. Dark clouds began to swirl in the sky overhead. Then something glowed inside the unnatural black clouds, and Chazz realized they were meteors of some kind, glowing red with an evil heat.

The meteors plummeted from the sky, pelting Chazz's Armed Dragon. It roared angrily as the meteors did their work, shattering the dragon.

And the Shadow Rider wasn't finished. He took a book with a leather cover from under his cloak. The Mark of Amnael glowed on the cover.

It's that mark again, but why? Chazz wondered.

The yellow seal rose from the book. At the same time, a fireball formed in the fist of the gigantic shadow monster behind the duelist.

The monster aimed the fireball at Chazz.

"Aaaaaah!" He cried out as the fireball took him down, draining his life points.

Jaden and the others heard the cry.

"Chazz!" Jaden yelled.

They ran toward the sound, and quickly reached the clearing. Chazz's cards floated on the water, and the Ojama Trio hovered above them, distraught.

"It's his cards!" Jaden said to his friends.

Deep under Academy Island, the Shadow Rider approached the lock to the Spirit Gates. Three of the locks had been opened by other Shadow Riders.

Now he had three more keys.

One by one, he placed each key into its stone lock. The locks lit up with an unearthly glow.

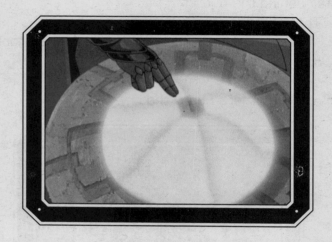

There was still one gate left to open, but the six open gates had an effect. Six thick beams of light erupted from the waters surrounding the island, shaking the island to its core.

Back in the woods, the ground trembled under Jaden's feet.

"What was that?" Syrus asked.

"Don't know," Jaden replied. "But definitely not a good thing!"

• CHAPTER TWELVE •

TIME TO SAVE THE WORLD

Chazz's head felt fuzzy. He slowly opened his eyes.

He wasn't sure where he was, but he knew he wasn't in the woods anymore. A strange, glittering mist swirled around him.

"Where am I?" he asked groggily.

As his eyes began to focus, he saw a figure floating in front of him. A girl in a white and blue uniform . . .

"Alexis?" Chazz wasn't sure, but it looked like she was inside some kind of weird bubble.

Then another bubble floated into his vision. This one held a sleeping boy.

"Atticus, too?" Chazz tried to sit up. "Where on Earth am I?"

Then Chazz realized he was floating around, too, just

like Alexis and Atticus. It almost looked like they were in space. Stars twinkled around them. And down below . . .

Chazz gasped. He could see a huge planet down below them, a blue planet with wispy clouds hovering in the atmosphere.

"Let's make that, where *off* Earth am I?" Chazz cried.

Miles and miles below, in the woods of Academy Island, Jaden, Syrus, and Chumley stared in awe at the six beams of light.

"What's going on around here?" Chumley asked. He clutched Professor Banner's cat, Pharaoh, in his arms.

"Yeah, those six laser beams of light just shot out of nowhere," Syrus said.

But Jaden had another thought. "You know what? I don't think they shot out from nowhere. I think they shot out from the Spirit Gates! Question is, how were they unlocked?"

Ojama Yellow appeared next to Jaden. "I'll tell you

how," said the little monster. "That seventh Shadow Rider is vicious!"

"You mean he took them all down?" Jaden asked in disbelief. "Chazz, Alexis, *and* Banner? But that would mean that . . ."

"That everyone's lost but Jaden," Syrus finished for him. "Jaden has the last key!"

"Oh man," Chumley groaned. "That seventh Shadow Rider must be really good!"

"No joke!" Syrus agreed. "Let's get out of here! This guy has got to be looking for you so he can unlock the final Spirit Gate. You have to hide immediately, before you end up like all the rest!" He shuddered as he imagined Jaden trapped in the clutches of the Shadow World.

"I'm not gonna hide, Sy," Jaden said firmly. "Our friends need our help, and we're going to give it to them — we have no choice!"

Syrus sighed. He hated to see Jaden in any danger. But he knew it was the only way. "Yeah, I guess you're right."

"Besides, we don't have to worry about this Shadow Rider guy finding me, because I plan on finding him first!" Jaden said boldly.

Chumley shivered with fear. "When you say 'I,' you don't mean 'we,' do ya?"

"You better believe I do!" Jaden said. "After all, it all comes down to this. Everything we've been working for. And I want you guys to be there when I beat this guy and we save the world!"

Jaden marched on into the woods. Syrus and Chumley exchanged glances, then followed him.

Not far away, in the basement of an old abandoned dorm, the mysterious Shadow Rider could sense Jaden's presence. He snickered behind his gray mask.

"All has gone according to plan," he said, his voice echoing through the dark basement. "All that remains is the endgame. Where Jaden will face a dueling trial unlike anything he's ever seen!"

CHAPTER THIRTEEN

A MYSTERIOUS MUMMY

The boys didn't get far before a jagged streak of lightning lit up the sky in front of them. The lightning zapped a nearby tree.

Craaaaack! The tree broke in two, and the top half toppled into a pond. The boys jumped back as the fallen tree narrowly missed hitting them.

"Uh, timber?" Jaden joked.

"That was way close," Syrus said, shuddering.

Then Jaden noticed something. "Hey, look!" he cried.

A glowing yellow symbol appeared on the trunk of the tree.

"The Mark of Amnael!" Chumley cried.

The symbol flashed, then appeared again over a trail in the woods.

"It's like it's trying to lead us someplace," Syrus pointed out.

"Not lishus," Chumley mumbled.

But Jaden was glad to see the mark. "Finding this guy's going to be easier than I thought!" he said. "Come on! Let's go!"

Syrus had his flashlight turned on, but the boys didn't really need it. The glowing Mark of Amnael led them through the woods. They followed the symbol until the trees thinned out a bit. Lightning flashed, illuminating a dilapidated building in front of them.

Jaden knew exactly where they were. "Makes sense," he said, remembering the story Atticus had told. "The abandoned dorm was where all of this started. It makes sense it would end here. Anyway, come on, guys. Let's keep moving!"

"Meeeeew!" Pharaoh squealed and jumped out of Chumley's arms. The cat ran straight into the old dorm.

Jaden followed Pharaoh, and Syrus and Chumley reluctantly did the same. Whatever had covered the walls had disintegrated long ago, leaving exposed wood beams and crumbling stone. There was no light except for Syrus's flashlight.

They walked down a narrow hallway, calling out Pharaoh's name. Finally, they came to a hole in the wall.

"Look! A passageway! And Pharaoh's paw prints," Chumley said, pointing.

"Well, we can't fit through that," Syrus said, sounding relieved. "Guess we'll have to turn around."

"Yeah, right, Sy. This way," Jaden said, turning around. Then he stopped. There was a door in the wall.

"That's weird," Jaden remarked. "That door wasn't there before."

Syrus laughed nervously. "So let's ignore it."

"Sounds good to me!" Chumley agreed.

Jaden ignored them both and walked through the door. Syrus and Chumley went in behind him.

They had entered some kind of large basement area. Industrial metal lights lit up the space with an eerie glow, but most of the basement was bathed in shadow. A pit on the floor had the markings of a duel arena on it. Chains and hooks hung from the ceiling.

"This place looks like some lab from a horror movie," Jaden said cheerfully.

"So, where's the mad scientist hiding?" Chumley asked nervously.

"Not sure. I just hope it's not where my gut tells me it might be," Syrus said.

Jaden was confused by his friend's remark until he

saw where Syrus was pointing his flashlight. A large stone coffin was propped up against the corner.

"A coffin!" Jaden cried.

"Or a refrigerator box?" Chumley suggested hopefully.

"Yeah, that's it," Syrus chimed in.

Jaden walked up to the coffin. "Chumley, give me a hand here," he said.

"Ah, sorry, Jay," Chumley said. "I'm only good at opening pickle jars and potato chip bags."

"He's not qualified, so why don't you just leave the coffin alone?" Syrus said.

"I bet he'd be qualified if this thing were filled with grilled cheese," Jaden joked.

Jaden pushed on the heavy stone lid with all his might. It took some doing, but he managed to slide it to the side.

A man in a white lab coat lay inside the coffin. His face was dried up and wrinkled, as though he had been dead for thousands of years. His wrinkled hands rested on his chest. His long hair was gray and brittle. Jaden noticed that he wore eyeglasses over his closed eyes.

"A mummy," Jaden said. "What's it doing here?"

The mummy really freaked out Syrus. "More like, what are *we* doing here?" he asked.

"Yeah, I'm with Sy on that one," Chumley agreed.

Something about the mummy bothered Jaden. "Give me your flashlight," he told Syrus.

"Why? What's wrong?" Syrus asked.

"What's wrong is that this mummy looks familiar,"

Jaden said, taking the flashlight from him. "There's only one way to be sure."

Jaden shone his flashlight on the mummy's white coat — the kind of coat worn by some professors at Duel Academy. A white ID card was sticking out of the pocket. Jaden gingerly pulled out the card. He read the name: Banner.

"It *is* him!" Jaden cried. "This is — or *was* — Professor Banner!"

"Professor Banner is the mummy?" Syrus was horrified.

"No way! Professor Banner couldn't have mummified this fast," Chumley pointed out. "I can't even make beef jerky in the amount of time he's been missing."

"So then, you think it's a fake?" Jaden asked.

"Of course! It's probably made out of wax or something," Syrus guessed.

"Wrong!" A strange, deep voice filled the basement. "That *is* the body of the one you know as Professor Banner."

"Who is that?" Jaden asked, turning around. He could hear the voice but couldn't see anyone.

A man stepped out of the shadows. He wore a gray mask and hood and a gray tunic and pants. A red sash was tied around his waist.

"The seventh Shadow Rider!" the man cried.

Ojama Yellow appeared next to Jaden.

"That's the one there!" he said, pointing. "He's the duelist that took down Chazz! And he's really good! But you gotta beat him to get Chazz back! You gotta!"

"It's true, Jaden," said the masked duelist. "To get any of your friends back, you'll have to beat me . . . Amnael."

"As in the Mark of Amnael, Amnael?" Jaden asked.

"That's right," Amnael said. He reached into his tunic and took out the book with the Mark of Amnael embossed on the cover. "And I have your friends right here."

Amnael held out the book and opened the cover.

Jaden wasn't sure exactly what happened next. It was as though there was a rip in time and space, and he could suddenly see his friends — Chazz, Alexis, and Atticus — floating through space in weird bubbles of some kind. Alexis and Atticus were barely conscious, but Chazz was pounding against the side of his bubble, screaming.

Then Amnael closed the book, and everything went back to normal.

"If you cannot defeat me, you will be joining them," Amnael warned. "All of you."

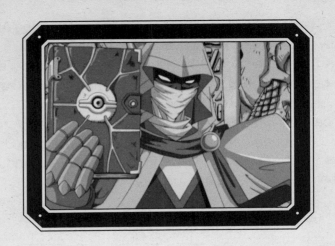

"But what about Professor Banner?" Jaden asked. "How do I get him back? Or is it too late?"

"It was *always* too late," Amnael said cryptically. "It is best that you forget the one you knew as Banner. He is no more."

"What do you mean, no more?" Jaden asked, his anger growing. "What is this? I want to know what you've done to Professor Banner!"

"To understand everything, you must do just one thing," Amnael said. He held up the book. "And that is, duel and defeat me, Jaden! Only then will the truth be revealed. Only then will this tome and the secrets it holds be unlocked. Will you accept this challenge? Will you face me?"

"No, I don't think so," Chumley answered.

Syrus nudged him. "Uh, he's talking to Jaden, Chumley."

"Of course I'll face you!" Jaden cried. He climbed down into the dueling pit.

"Be careful!" Syrus called out.

"Let's throw down!" Jaden challenged, looking Amnael directly in the eyes. He activated his Duel Disk.

Amnael activated his Duel Disk next. "Prepare yourself!" he called out. Then he lowered his hood to reveal a head of long, white hair. The dark gray mask still covered his face.

"I've been preparing for this ever since you Shadow Riders first showed!" Jaden called back. "And now, Amnael . . . get your game on!"

CHAPTER FOURTEEN

AMNAEL'S ALCHEMY BEASTS

Jaden and Amnael both drew their cards.

"I'm getting my friends back!" Jaden called out. "No matter what it takes, Amnael!"

"Is that so?" the Shadow Rider replied. "But what if you do not possess what it takes, Jaden? Because to beat me, you'll have to reach a whole new echelon of dueling expertise."

Jaden set his mouth in a grim line. Amnael could talk all the trash he wanted. It wasn't going to effect him.

"Now we begin!" Amnael's deep voice boomed across the dueling field. "And I activate the spell card Chaos Distill!"

Amnael held up the card, and a huge machine of shining metal rose up behind him. A globe-shaped tank sat on metal legs. Pipes and hoses snaked around the outside of the tank, and glass windows revealed a steamy, bubbling liquid inside.

"What *is* that thing?" Syrus wondered.

"Oh yeah, like *I'm* gonna know," Chumley replied.

"Due to its effect, all my cards that would normally go to the graveyard in this duel will instead be removed from play!" Amnael announced.

This puzzled Jaden. *Why would he want his cards removed from play?* He kept the thought to himself.

"Now I'll activate my second spell card, Steel Lamp!" Amnael continued. "And when Chaos Distill is on the field, I can use Steel Lamp to summon Alchemy Beast Salamandra the Steel!"

Amnael held up the card, which showed a picture of a metal lantern. The card was whisked into Chaos Distill, and a glowing mist covered it. Then a steel dragon with huge wings and a long tail appeared in front of Amnael.

"You see, Alchemy Beasts can't be summoned in the normal manner, but they *can* wage direct attacks against you," Amnael said. "Which is a big problem. Because with these two spell cards, Bronze Scale and Lead Compass, along with Chaos Distill, I can now summon two more Alchemy Beasts!"

The two spell cards vanished into Chaos Distill.

"Ouroboros the Bronze!" Amnael cried, and a serpentlike creature with three eyes on the side of its head appeared.

"Leon the Lead!" A gray creature that looked like a lion with yellow eyes appeared.

The three Alchemy Beasts stood in front of Amnael, roaring, hissing, and growling. They each had 500 attack points.

"Three monsters in the very first turn?" Jaden remarked. He had never faced an opponent like Amnael before.

"That is correct," Amnael said. "And if you think that is impressive, just wait until you see them attack!"

"I'm not going to give them that chance!" Jaden cried. "I summon Hero Bubbleman!"

A hero in a blue uniform with a bubble tank strapped to his back came on the field. Bubbleman had 800 attack points.

"And since he's the only one out, I get to draw two more cards," Jaden continued. "And I have a feeling they're going to be some sweet ones!"

Jaden drew the cards and grinned. "It's good to be right! I activate Bubble Blaster!"

A giant bubble cannon appeared in Bubbleman's

arms. His attack points immediately rose to 1600 — more than enough to take down the Alchemy Beasts.

"Fire, Bombarding Bubble Barage!" Jaden yelled.

"That is one bubble that I'm afraid I must burst," Amnael said. "I activate a trap: Elemental Absorber!"

Amnael's facedown card flipped up, and the image of a strange device appeared in the middle of the field. It was black, and shaped like the top half of a globe. Black spikes jutted out of its top. The flat bottom sat atop an inverted black cone.

"With this card, I can remove a monster in my hand from play to negate the attack of your monster as long as they both have the same attribute," Amnael explained. He reached for a card in his hand.

"Not good," Jaden said.

"No, it's not. Not when the card I remove from play is Aqua Spirit!" Amnael cried.

Jaden cringed. Aqua Spirit was a Water Attribute card — just like Bubbleman.

Bubbleman aimed the Bubble Blaster at Amnael, sending a powerful surge of bubbles across the field. But the Elemental Absorber began to spin. A giant wave appeared on the field, pushing back Bubbleman and his bubbles.

"No, my attack!" Jaden cried.

"Has been stopped," Amnael said firmly. "It's my turn now! Go, my Alchemy Beasts! Attack Jaden directly! Salamandra of Steel, let loose Flameshot of Ore!"

The metal dragon opened its mouth, and a hot ball of flame began to form there. With a mighty roar, Salamandra sent the fireball shooting across the field.

"Now, Ouroboros and Leon attack as well!" Amnael commanded.

Metal projectiles exploded from the mouth of the serpent, and Leon sent a ball of blue energy hurling from its huge mouth.

Slam! Slam! Slam! The attacks hit Jaden one after the other. He moaned as his life points dropped down to 2500.

Syrus gasped. "Jaden just got clobbered!"

"Hang in there, Jaden!" Chumley called out. "Amnael's only got one card left in his hand! If you can hold on through this turn, you'll have the upper hand, and *he'll* be the one who's on the ropes!"

Amnael snickered. "Is that what you think? You should have paid better attention in class. Perhaps then you would know that against my alchemy deck, things are not what they seem. I activate the spell card Black Process Negledo!"

He held up the card, which showed a pattern of colored triangles.

"When Chaos Distill is on the field and there are no cards in my hand, this card allows me to remove all Alchemy Beasts on the field from play, and then draw two new cards per beast!" As Amnael announced this, the three Alchemy Beasts shattered and disappeared in a wall of flames.

"So then, you're taking out your own monsters?" Jaden asked.

"That is the way of the alchemist: destruction and rebirth," Amnael explained. "But I assure you, if you are destroyed here, there will be no rebirth for *you*!"

Jaden clenched his fists tightly.

"Now then, since I removed three Alchemy Beasts from play, I get to draw six cards," Amnael continued. He drew the cards. "Let's play some of them. I activate Tin Spell Circle, Mercury Hourglass, and Silver Key!"

The spell cards were transported into the distiller, and three new Alchemy Beasts appeared, each with 500 attack points. Aretos the Tin looked like an eagle made of metal. Ekanus the Mercury was a shining shark creature. And Moonface the Silver was a moon with long legs and arms sticking out of its head.

Jaden took a deep breath. "All right, now it's my turn. Go, Elemental Hero Clayman!"

Clayman appeared with his 800 attack points.

"Next I'll play the spell card Mud Max!" Jaden cried. An all-terrain vehicle appeared on the field. "That puts Clayman in overdrive to the tune of 300 extra supercharged attack points!"

Clayman jumped inside Mud Max, and his attack points rose to 1100.

"Oh, and guess what, Amnael! I'm going to use them

now to run over your life points," Jaden said. "So hit it, Clayman. Put the pedal to the metal and attack!"

But Amnael had a counter. "I activate the effect of Elemental Absorber! By simply removing the Rock Spirit from play, I can negate the attack of that Earth Attribute monster!"

Amnael took Rock Spirit from his hand and removed it from play. The Elemental Absorber began to spin once again. Clayman charged across the field in Mud Max, but a mountain of rock rose in front of him, stopping his attack.

"Oh man," Jaden groaned. "It's like he has a card to cancel every attribute monster in my deck."

"I warned you, Jaden," said Amnael. "To be triumphant you will need to use your cards in a way you've never used them before. You will need to become a better duelist than you've ever been. If not, you will join your friends."

"Oh, I'll be joining my friends, all right," Jaden said. "When I free them!"

"Then you had better 'get your game on,' because

you have already fallen far behind," Amnael replied. "And you're about to fall even farther!"

Amnael held up another card with colored triangles on it. "I activate the spell card White Process Albedo," he said. "And thanks to it, I can now summon Golden Homonculus!"

Flames leapt up on the field, and a giant creature began to take form. Golden Homonculus was a giant made of gold, a huge powerhouse that towered over every human and monster on the field.

"Forged in fire, Golden Homonculus doesn't work like any other card you've seen," Amnael said proudly. "You see, his attack points and defense points are equal to the number of cards that I've removed from play and then multiplied by 300! So, since I have removed thirteen cards so far, his attack points become 3900!"

Jaden gasped. That was some monster!

Amnael's dark eyes glittered across the field.

"And your life points are about to become zero!" he cried.

◆ CHAPTER FIFTEEN ◆

A SHOCKING SURPRISE!

"It is over, Jaden. And I was expecting so much more from you," Amnael said. He sounded disappointed. "Attack, Alchemy Beasts!"

The three monsters attacked Jaden together. Aretos the Tin shot flames from its back. Ekenas the Mercury sent waves of pulsating blue light across the field. And Moonface the Silver sent small and sharp crescents flying toward Jaden.

"Aaaaaaaah!" Jaden cried out as the attacks hit their mark. His attack points plummeted to 1000.

"But I'm not finished yet," said Amnael. "Now, Golden Homonculus, attack! Stone Shard Storm!"

Homonculus roared and flexed his huge arms. Sharp

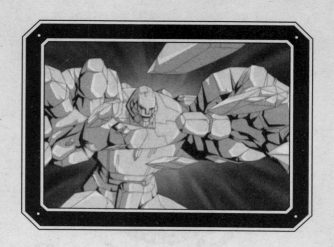

shards of gold catapulted across the field, slamming into Jaden and his heroes. A cloud of dust rose up, covering them, as the shards hit their marks.

"You are beaten!" Amnael boomed.

But as the dust cleared, another sound was heard in the basement — the sound of Jaden's laughter. He was still standing — and so were Clayman and Bubbleman. Only Mud Max was gone.

"Hate to disappoint you, but I'm still here!" Jaden said, grinning. "Know why? Because when you attacked, I used the effect of my equip spell, Mud Max. Now by destroying it, your attack's canceled out!"

Amnael growled behind his mask.

"But hold on, Amnael, there's something else," Jaden went on. "Some*one*, rather. Because I also get to summon an Elemental Hero, and I'm bringing out Avian!"

Avian burst out onto the field, flexing his huge, white wings; 1000 attack points flashed next to the hero.

"Impressive," Amnael said grudgingly.

"I'm not done," Jaden said. "Now I'm going to play Elemental Hero Burstinatrix!"

Jaden's red-clad hero appeared, her long, black hair streaming behind her. With 1200 attack points, she was one of Jaden's strongest heroes.

"Now let's use some of these monsters," Jaden said. "Go, Avian! Attack with Quill Cascade!"

Avian sent a shower of white feathers across the field, but Amnael was ready for him.

"Go, Elemental Absorber!" he yelled. "I remove Garuda the Wind Spirit to negate your attack!"

The Elemental Absorber spun around, and a wind sprung up that pushed back all of Avian's feathers.

Jaden frowned. It was almost as though Amnael knew what cards were in his deck and had prepared to counter each one of them.

"And since another card has been removed from the game, the attack points of Golden Homonculus increase!" Amnael cried. His huge monster's points jumped to 4200.

"Yeah, yeah," Jaden said. "Burstinatrix, Flare Storm!"

Burstinatrix held out her arm, and a huge red fireball formed in her hand. She hurled it across the field in one long, blazing stream.

Amnael held up another card. "I remove Spirit of Flames to negate your attack. Go, Elemental Absorber!"

The strange black object spun once more, and a wall of flames sprung up that blocked Burstinatrix's attack.

Syrus shook his head. "Aw, man. Nothing's getting through to do damage!"

"I know. That Elemental Absorber keeps canceling out his attacks," Chumley agreed.

Jaden shrugged. "It's cool! I guess I'll just have to use something other than my Elemental Heroes, then! So I'm going to play Burst Return. When Burstinatrix is on the field, this card lets me return all other Elemental Heroes back to my hand. Time to come on back, you guys!"

Clayman, Bubbleman, and Avian vanished from the field as Jaden put the cards back in his hand.

Then Jaden held up another card. "Next I'll activate the spell card Burst Impact! Now all monsters out other than Burstinatrix are destroyed! And then you take three hundred points of damage for each of them!"

A blue protective light glowed around Burstinatrix.

"Now go, Burst Impact!" Jaden yelled.

Burstinatrix hurled another blazing fireball across the field.

Boom! The tin eagle shattered.

Boom! The mercury shark exploded.

Boom! The silver moon disintegrated.

BOOM! The huge Homonculus erupted into millions of tiny shards.

Amnael tried to protect himself from the blast. His life points dropped to 2800, and his mask cracked.

"Yeah!" Chumley cheered.

"Way to play, Jay!" Syrus added. "I *knew* he'd turn this duel around sooner or later."

Just then, Pharaoh the cat ran up to Syrus's feet.

"You here to help Jaden?" Syrus asked. "Great! You can watch with me."

Syrus picked up Pharaoh, and the cat scratched him in the face with his sharp claws.

"Owwww!" Syrus cried.

Pharaoh yowled and jumped out of Syrus's arms. The cat ran across the field — right toward Amnael!

"No, Pharaoh!" Jaden called out. "That guy's dangerous!"

But Pharaoh didn't seem to think so. He rubbed up against the Shadow Rider's legs, purring.

"But Pharaoh's *never* friendly with strangers," Chumley said, puzzled.

"Chumley's right," Jaden said, and a thought was slowly dawning on him. "Then, Amnael . . ."

"Is no stranger," the Shadow Rider finished for him. "To Pharaoh. Or to you!"

Amnael took off his mask to reveal a pale, scarred face. A face they had all seen before.

"Professor Banner?" Chumley asked in disbelief.

"Wait, if you're Banner, then who's that mummy?" Jaden asked.

Banner laughed. "That mummy is also me," he said. He knelt down and picked up Pharaoh. "Oh, my children, there is more going on here than you could possibly imagine!"

Jaden, Chumley, and Syrus stared at Banner in frozen silence. How could their beloved professor, a Key Keeper, be a Shadow Rider? And a mummy, too? It was all too much to take in.

Banner slowly stroked Pharaoh's back, smiling. "The truth will be revealed soon enough!"